VALENTINO PIER

W9-BNX-721

REED FARREL COLEMAN

RAVEN BOOKS
an imprint of
ORCA BOOK PUBLISHERS

Library and Archives Canada Cataloguing in Publication

Coleman, Reed Farrel, 1956-
Valentino Pier / Reed Farrel Coleman.
(Rapid Reads)

Issued also in electronic formats.
ISBN 978-1-4598-0209-4

I. Title. II. Series: Rapid reads
PS3553.O47443V35 2013   813'.54   C2013-901878-6

First published in the United States, 2013
Library of Congress Control Number: 2013935304

Summary: PI Gulliver Dowd rescues a street kid's dog,
but when the kid is found badly beaten the next day,
Gulliver uncovers a new mystery. (RL 2.5)

MIX
Paper from
responsible sources
FSC® C016245
www.fsc.org

*Orca Book Publishers is dedicated to preserving the environment and has
printed this book on Forest Stewardship Council® certified paper.*

Orca Book Publishers gratefully acknowledges the support for
its publishing programs provided by the following agencies:
the Government of Canada through the Canada Book Fund and the
Canada Council for the Arts, and the Province of British Columbia
through the BC Arts Council and the Book Publishing Tax Credit.

Design by Teresa Bubela
Cover photography by Getty Images

ORCA BOOK PUBLISHERS
PO Box 5626, Stn. B
Victoria, BC Canada
V8R 6S4

ORCA BOOK PUBLISHERS
PO Box 468
Custer, WA USA
98240-0468

www.orcabook.com
Printed and bound in Canada.

16 15 14 13 • 4 3 2 1

To Ezra

CHAPTER ONE

Gulliver Dowd had one new message on his cell. His guts knotted up as he listened. The woman was panicked. He could hear it in her voice. It was a voice he knew too well. One he had hoped he would never hear again. The woman's daughter was gone. He had warned her this would happen. And it had.

Nina Morton's voice was cracking now. She was crying. Begging for Dowd's help. He had found her daughter once. He could do it again. She just knew he could. He could do anything when he put his mind to it. Hadn't he become a licensed private investigator? Hadn't he earned his black belt? Hadn't he become a dead shot? All of this in spite of his deformed body. And Nina swore she would do anything for him. Even marry him if that's what he wanted. All he had to do was find Anka again. Gulliver stopped listening. He erased the message.

It wasn't that Gulliver's heart didn't ache. It did. It ached all the time. It would ache for Nina until the day he died. But sometimes you can't save people from themselves. Nina was like that. She had been Gulliver's high school girlfriend for two months. Those were the best two months of his life. The names people called him didn't matter. *Midget. Runt. Dwarf. Freak.* They couldn't hurt him. Not as long as she was in love with him. He was Superman as long as he had Nina. It didn't last. Gulliver knew that nothing good ever lasts.

That was eighteen years ago. He had spent seventeen of those years hoping Nina would come back to him. And last year she had. Presto! Like magic. Black magic. She had betrayed Gulliver. She had betrayed her daughter. She had betrayed herself. And now the girl was gone again. Gulliver didn't think the girl would ever be back. But he took no joy in being right. He took no joy in Nina's loss. He knew what it was like to lose someone forever. No one deserves that kind of pain.

His mind went to Keisha. She was gone too. Forever. People don't come back from the grave. He had been so proud of his adopted sister when she graduated from the police academy. He looked at Keisha's picture in the frame on his desk. Her beautiful black skin. Her fierce eyes. Her wary smile. All set against her dress blue uniform. Then he remembered seeing her in the morgue. Cold. Dead. Lost to him. He still didn't get how it had all gone so wrong. How could someone murder a cop in cold blood? How could they do it in broad daylight? How could seven years go by without the killer being caught? How? How? How? Gulliver had asked himself these same questions every day. He got no answers. But it never stopped him. He would find her killer some day. He would never give up. Never. It's what kept him going.

Now he was crying, his tears bitter as lemon juice. His squat body shook. Sometimes Keisha's murder made him angry. So angry he could explode. Days like today, he was just sad. Sad for Keisha. Sad for himself. When he was like this, there was only one thing to do. Gulliver dialed Steven Mandel's work number. He and Mandel had known each other since they were little kids. Each was the other's best friend. Gulliver's only real friend.

"What's up, Gullie?" asked Mandel.

"Have a drink with me tonight, Rabbi." Gulliver had always called Steven that. He wasn't sure why. But it fit. Steven was wise and loving. He always had been.

"Can't. Business. You sound weird. Are you okay?"

"Fine," Gulliver lied. He did that sometimes. Lied. In that way he was like everybody else. Not much else about him was.

He had to get out of his loft. The walls were closing in on him. He wasn't much of a walker. With short legs. Uneven legs. He wobbled. At least they knew him around Red Hook. No one pointed. The local kids didn't giggle. Not anymore. He was like a crack in the sidewalk that everyone had gotten used to.

Gulliver looked up and down Visitation Place. Red Hook was quiet. Kids were in school. It was a day that said winter was finally gone. The sky was so blue it almost didn't look real. There wasn't a cloud anywhere. The sun was strong and warm on his face. Gulliver's face. That was God's cruel joke. God had built him out of spare parts. Mismatched parts. But he had given Gulliver Dowd a handsome face.

A mild breeze blew in off the harbor. It smelled of the salt from the ocean. That's what got his attention.

He hobbled along Van Brunt. Down Van Dyke. He ran out of street at Valentino Pier. The pier was a finger of concrete that stuck out into New York Harbor. It was named for a hero fireman. A dead hero. There was no shortage of those in New York City.

Gulliver liked it here. The view was amazing. At the end of the pier, the Statue of Liberty stared back at him. To his left, the Verrazano-Narrows Bridge. Staten Island. New Jersey. To his right was Lower Manhattan. The new Freedom Tower rose up above all else. Keisha said she had watched the World Trade Center towers fall from the pier.

It was an odd day. A day to recall sad things. But also a day to take a step back. A day to watch tugboats. Water taxis. Ocean liners. Helicopters. Seagulls. A day to lose yourself in the rush of the harbor. He needed to lose himself. He had been busy lately. He hadn't slept much. He'd spent weeks in Boston working an art-theft case. He'd gotten the paintings back. And a nice finder's fee from the insurance company.

Gulliver had once worked almost all missing-children cases. Not anymore. Not in the year since he had found Nina's daughter, Anka. Nina had lied to Gulliver. She'd told him Anka was *his* daughter too. He was crushed when he found out it wasn't true. That Anka was someone else's girl. After that he couldn't handle missing-children cases. It hurt too much. The wound was still too fresh. He was thinking about Anka. How pretty she was. How smart she was. How talented. How for a few days she had been his. That's when he felt a tap on his shoulder. He turned around.

"Yo, mister. You seen my dog?"

The boy was maybe ten years old. He was already four inches taller than Gulliver.

But he was a skinny kid. A street kid. Gulliver knew the signs. A dirty face. Crooked teeth. Underfed. Untamed Faraway eyes. Nervous like a cat. Ready to pounce or to run. Gulliver had spent a lot of time with kids just like this boy. Runaways ended up on the street sooner or later. Even the ones with money would find out it doesn't last too long. When the money runs out, there's only one place to land. The street. Gulliver often started his searches for runaways on the street. This kid was different. He wasn't a runaway. He didn't end up on the street. He came from the street.

"What kind of dog is it?" Gulliver asked.

He shrugged his shoulders. "A dog dog. I don't know what kind."

"Big or little?"

"Kinda little, I guess. He's this long." The kid held his hands about a foot apart. "And he's this tall." He held one hand a foot above the other. "He got kinda a scrunchy black face. His eyes go this way and that. And he don't smell too good. He got brown and black fur and some white."

"What's his name?"

"Ugly."

Gulliver laughed. "Your dog's name is Ugly? I like that."

The kid smiled. It was a nice smile, in spite of his crooked teeth. But a wary smile, like Keisha's. Keisha had been in foster care before Gulliver's parents adopted her. Love and trust didn't come easy to her. Love and trust didn't come easy to street kids either.

"How long has Ugly been missing?"

"Two days."

Gulliver wanted to ask the kid a thousand questions. Where were his parents? Had he ever gone to school? Where did he sleep? When did he last eat? But he only asked simple questions. Ones that wouldn't spook the kid. He knew that once he started asking hard questions, the kid would take off.

"My name's Gulliver Dowd. I live at Visitation Place. You can ask people about me. They'll tell you I'm okay."

"I know. I seen you around. You're the little man that finds people."

"I find lots of things," Gulliver said. "Maybe even dogs."

The kid smiled again. "I miss Ugly."

"I bet he misses you too. Where did you see him last?"

"Over by Coffey Park. He saw a squirrel or something and took off after it. I followed him. He's ugly, but he's fast."

Gulliver reached into his pants pocket. "I'm going to get my wallet out and give you my card. Okay?"

The kid stopped smiling.

Gulliver thought he knew why. "It's okay if you can't read. You'll learn. There's lots of things I learned when I was old already. No one thought I could learn them, but I did."

The kid pumped up his chest. "I can read. It's just that the letters get all crazy sometimes."

Like this kid's life wasn't already hard enough. "Here's my card and twenty dollars."

That set off alarm bells. "What's the money for?"

"For food. Some for you. Some for Ugly. You can pay me back someday after I find your dog. Deal?" Gulliver held out his hand to the kid.

The kid took it and shook it. "Deal."

Gulliver wagged his finger at the kid and winked. "Go get something to eat. Check with me tomorrow."

The kid turned and ran. It was only a few seconds later that it hit Gulliver. He didn't know the kid's name. He shouted after him. Too late. The kid was gone.

CHAPTER TWO

Coffey Park was down the block from Gulliver's loft. The apartment had been his sister's. He'd moved in after she was killed. He felt closer to Keisha there. And he liked Red Hook. It was once a tough place. Toughest in Brooklyn. Toughest in all of New York City. Not anymore. Now it was filled with hipsters and young families. But it was still a bit rough around the edges.

Gulliver stopped at a bodega before going after the kid's dog. He bought a half-pound of rare roast beef. He figured that Ugly hadn't eaten much in the last few days. Much easier to make friends with a strange dog when you have food to offer. And he knew that the dog would be like the kid. Nervous. Untrusting. Maybe a little scared.

The park was busy. Young mothers gathered in groups. Their kids were on swings. Playing tag. Coming to life with the early spring. Some old men were playing chess. They had gray stubble on their stern faces. But even they smiled at the warmth of the sun. At the blue skies. The basketball courts were alive with action. They always were. Even late into the night. This was Brooklyn. Basketball was like a religion in Brooklyn. The hand-ball courts were busy too. Kids cut school. No shock in that. Days like this were made for cutting class.

He made his way to the basketball courts. He loved watching the kids play hoops. They were like young horses in a field. Full of energy and fire. Both awkward and graceful. There was nothing graceful about Gulliver. Sure, he had earned his black belt. He was swift with a knife. He could draw his Sig 9mm before you could snap your fingers. But his movements were herky-jerky. He could be quick. Not smooth.

There was a familiar face on the other side of the court. Heyman Jones was a Brooklyn basketball legend. In the 1970s he was All-City three years at Boys High School. Played his college ball at NC State. First round NBA pick. But he ruined his knees. It's hard to be a power forward with bad knees. He lasted only four years in the pros. For the last twenty years he had been a college scout for the Knicks. But what Heyman really enjoyed was watching the kids. Gulliver waved to him. Heyman nodded and came around the fence.

Everyone towered over Gulliver. At six foot eleven, Heyman towered over everyone. He and Gulliver were a funny pair standing next to each other. Heyman had a shaved head and a full gray beard.

"Hey, Dowd."

"Heyman. How are you?"

"Good."

"These kids have any future?" Gulliver asked.

"The skinny white boy's got some game. And the little brother with the ball now. He got more handling skills than some college kids. The rest are just okay."

Gulliver looked way up at Heyman. He liked watching Heyman watch. Heyman's dark brown eyes lit up when he watched.

Gulliver said, "You been around the park all morning?"

"Uh-huh, all morning. Lots of ball on days like this."

"You happen to see an ugly little dog? Pushed-in black face?"

"Got some ratty black and brown fur? Kinda looks like a cross between an alien and a Pug? That dog stinks, man," Heyman answered. "Why you wanna know?"

"I'm working my first missing-dog case."

Heyman laughed a deep, rich laugh. "He was over by the garden. Good luck with that. He's a nasty little pup. Growling at me and all."

"Later, Heyman."

"Later, little man."

Gulliver didn't like being called *little man*. But since everyone was a *little man* to Heyman Jones, it was okay. The only other person Gulliver let call him *little man* was Ahmed Foster. Ahmed was an ex-Navy Seal from Gulliver's old town on Long Island. They had reconnected at Keisha's funeral. Ahmed and Keisha had once dated. Ahmed had taught Gulliver knife fighting. He also helped out on cases. But Gulliver didn't think he would need Ahmed for this case. He was sure the roast beef would do the trick.

He moved away from the courts to where Heyman said he had seen Ugly. There was a beautiful garden in the park.

In a few weeks, all sorts of flowers would be blooming. Tight green buds were already showing. Bees would be buzzing. The days would get warmer and warmer. Gulliver closed his eyes for a second. He was remembering the first time Keisha had brought him to this park.

Look at that garden, Gullie, she'd said. *Roses. Tulips and all. Just like Mom's. And it's in the middle of a city park.*

Keisha was like that. Fierce as she was. As rough a life as she had. She could see beauty in things. Not Gulliver. He had an uneasy time with beauty. Until Keisha's death he had never even looked for beauty. Now he tried to see things the way his sister had.

Something got his attention. He couldn't decide whether he noticed the odor or the growling first. It didn't matter. Because when he opened his eyes, Gulliver knew he had solved the case. The ugliest and smelliest dog he had ever met was only a few feet away.

"The kid wasn't lying," he said to the dog. "You are ugly, Ugly. And you need a bath."

"You ain't no prize either," the dog's look seemed to say.

Smart dog, Gulliver thought. He took out his iPhone. He searched for the closest dog-grooming salon or veterinary clinic. There was a vet that also offered grooming only a few blocks away. Now he had to figure out how to get Ugly there. He wanted to help the kid out. But he didn't want to get bitten. Then he remembered the roast beef.

Gulliver dropped small pieces of beef behind him as he hobbled to the vet's. Ugly might have been ugly. Ugly might have been smelly. But Ugly wasn't stupid. And he was hungry. They got into the waiting room of the clinic with a slice of roast beef to spare. Gulliver could only imagine what the vet tech thought when they came in. The circus freak and the world's least lovable dog. She kept looking from Gulliver to Ugly and back again.

Gulliver shrugged. "Check the dog out. Do whatever you have to to make sure he's healthy," he said. He placed his credit card on the counter. "Then groom him."

Now it was the vet tech's turn to shrug *her* shoulders. "I'm not sure grooming's gonna help that much. He's pretty ugly." She giggled. "Sorry."

"Don't apologize. I'm short, not blind. He's so ugly his name is Ugly."

She laughed again. "Okay...Gulliver," she said, reading his name from the credit card. "We'll do what we can. Give us a few hours. Here's some paperwork for you."

He read her name tag. "Thank you...Mia."

She smiled at him. It was a shy smile. Not an innocent one. It had been a long time since a woman had smiled at him that way. He didn't know what to do about it. So he just took the paperwork and got busy writing.

CHAPTER THREE

Gulliver's parents had adopted children, not animals. Sharing his loft with Ugly for the night was as close as Gulliver had ever come to having a pet. One night. That's as long as he figured to hang on to the mutt. No doubt the kid would be by in the morning to see if he'd found the dog. Then he would give Ugly back to his master. He figured finding the dog would earn him some respect. Buy him some time to talk to the kid. Time to ask him the hard questions he hadn't asked before. At least he could slip the kid some more money.

The dog was asleep on a blanket. He'd had a rough day. The vet had given him vaccinations against all sorts of diseases. Pumped him full of medicines to treat the ones he already had. Even cleaned his teeth. They'd shaved his old fur down to the skin. Flea-dipped him. Bathed him. And bathed him again. Gulliver had to admit the dog smelled a lot better. But even with his ratty fur gone. With clean teeth. The pooch was still as ugly as could be.

Gulliver was half-asleep on the couch. The TV was on. There was a knock at the door. Ugly didn't like that. He stirred. Walked to the door. Growled a low, steady growl. Gulliver didn't like it either. It was nearly three o'clock in the morning. And you had to ring the loft from the lobby. Then you had to wait to be buzzed in. Gulliver wrapped his oddly shaped hand around the butt of his Sig. Then relaxed. It must be the kid, he thought. Probably couldn't wait to see if Gulliver had found his dog. Street kids don't live by the clock. They also have ways of getting into places without following the rules. The street has its own rules.

"One second," he called out. He pulled back the door.

It wasn't the kid. Of course it wasn't. The dog wouldn't be growling if it was the kid. But what did Gulliver know about dogs? Two big men stood in the doorway. Both had blue-and-gold NYPD detective shields hanging from their jacket pockets. One of them looked familiar. He was in his forties. He had thinning reddish hair. Some of it was gray. Blue eyes. A sad mouth. Gulliver couldn't remember where he knew the detective from. The other guy was a blob. Fat. Double-chinned. Bald. Older. Cold gray eyes in tiny slits.

"You Dowd?" the red-haired detective asked.

"Gulliver Dowd. Yes. Why?"

"We'll ask the questions," said the Blob.

"I'm Detective Sam Patrick. This is my partner, Detective Rigo." He nodded at the Blob.

"What can I do for you, detectives?" Gulliver asked. Then he turned to Ugly. "Go back to your blanket and lie down." The dog listened. Nestled back down on his blanket. But kept his bulging eyes on the cops.

"Ugly dog," Rigo said.

That pissed Gulliver off. "You always this pleasant? I wonder what the dog thinks about your weight."

"Listen, you little freak. I'm gonna—"

"Enough," snapped Patrick. He held out a plastic bag. "Is this your card?"

Gulliver took the bag. One of his business cards was inside. It had specks of red on it. His heart thumped in his chest. "Yeah. It's mine. Where did you find it?"

"It was recovered from a crime scene an hour ago."

Gulliver felt like he'd been punched in the gut. "Oh, shit. The kid. It's the kid, right?

About ten? Skinny? Dirty T-shirt? Crooked teeth? About this tall?" He held his hand a few inches above his head. "Dark brown eyes?"

The Blob said, "We don't know about his eyes. They was shut at the time."

"Is he—"

"Nah," Patrick said. "He's not dead. He's hurt bad though. They don't know how bad yet. He's at Brooklyn University Hospital."

The Blob poked Gulliver in the chest. "Why'd you do it, Dowd?"

"Do what?" Gulliver turned to Patrick. "Tell your partner that if he does that again, I'll break his fingers."

"I'd like to see you try." Rigo went to poke him again. "You little—"

Gulliver grabbed the fat detective's thumb. Twisted it. Rigo fell to his knees. He was red-faced. He winced in pain.

"Now that we see eye to eye, Detective Rigo..."

"You're assaulting an officer," Rigo said through gritted teeth.

Patrick laughed. Then commanded, "Let him go, Dowd. Now!"

Gulliver let go of the fat man's hand. Rigo got to his feet. He rubbed the feeling back into his hand.

"How did this kid come to have your card on him?" Patrick asked.

"He was my client."

Rigo snorted. "Get outta here."

Gulliver pointed over his shoulder with his thumb. "That's the kid's dog. He asked me to find the dog. I found the dog. I knew he was a street kid. No home. No phone. I gave him my card so he could check in with me. I thought it was the kid at the door just now. You can ask Juan at the bodega on Van Brunt. Heyman Jones at Coffey Park. And Mia at Dr. Prentice's vet clinic on Union Street. They'll tell you I spent the day looking for and taking care of the dog. There's a video camera outside the building that will tell you when I came into the building. It will show you I haven't left since."

"And you did this thing with the dog out of the goodness of your heart?" Patrick asked.

"Yeah. I was sad today. I was missing my—" Gulliver stopped midsentence. He suddenly remembered how he knew Detective Patrick. "You used to be in uniform at the Seven-Five in East New York. Didn't you?"

Patrick tilted his head. "That's right. But how—"

Gulliver had spent many days at the Seven-Five precinct house in the year after his sister's murder. And he never forgot faces. He turned. Went to his desk. Got the picture of Keisha in her dress blues. He showed the framed photo to the detectives. "That's my sister, Keisha," he said.

Rigo shook his head and laughed. "You got some strange genes in your family. A dwarf and a—"

"That's enough, Rigo," Patrick shouted at his partner. "I'll handle this. Go wait in the car."

"Suit yourself," he said. Turned. Went down the steps.

"Keisha was a good cop," Patrick said when he was sure Rigo was gone. "That was a bad day when they found her like that."

"All I've had are bad days since then. Come in. Tell me what happened to the kid."

Detective Patrick sat down on the couch across from the desk. Gulliver handed him a beer. He had one himself. That thing about cops not drinking on duty is bullshit.

"Found him behind an ocean freight container on Ferris Street near Valentino Pier. Looks like someone whacked him pretty good across the side of his head. The kid had your card folded in his hand. He also had a twenty-dollar bill in his pocket."

Gulliver explained about giving the kid the bill. About what he told the kid to do with the money. About how he found the dog. About how he had dealt with a lot of street kids. "I didn't even know the kid's name. He looked like he needed some help. I figured once he came for the dog I would be able to talk to him. Find out about his folks. See if I could get him some real help."

Patrick put his half-empty beer down on the floor. "Okay, Dowd. Come in tomorrow. Give us an official statement. Maybe by then we'll know something."

Gulliver was curious. "What's the kid's name?"

"Maybe that's one of the things we'll know by tomorrow."

"Is he gonna make it?"

"That's another thing we might know," Patrick said, winking at Gulliver. "Hope so.

Otherwise you'll be stuck with that ugly mutt."

"Or he'll be stuck with me. No bargain anyway you look at it."

CHAPTER FOUR

The weather had turned. But that's spring in New York. Blue skies one day, gray the next. Gulliver took Ugly with him to the precinct house. They made a funny pair. Gulliver laughed at some of the looks they got.

"You and me," Gulliver said to Ugly. "Two runts of their litters."

As they walked, Gulliver came to see just how lucky Ugly was. The dog wasn't aware he was ugly. Girl dogs probably didn't care about his squished-in face. His stubby little legs. His bulging eyeballs. His bent tail. Words couldn't hurt him.

Not the way they hurt Gulliver. Ugly just lived his life from day to day. From meal to meal. And he was loved. That kid really loved his dog. What Gulliver wouldn't give to be loved.

He gave his statement as he had promised he would. Then he had a talk with Detective Patrick. Gulliver was glad that Detective Rigo was nowhere in sight.

"Any word on the kid?" he asked.

Patrick said, "Still unconscious, but stable."

"That's something."

"He's been in the system. Name is Ellis Torres. Mother's a tweaker. In and out of jail and rehab all the time. Right now she's doing a short bid for a parole violation. The father…he's in the wind."

"So the kid really is on his own."

Patrick smiled, looking to the dog. "Yeah. Him and the mutt. They put the kid in foster care when the mother went away. Ran after a few days."

"No surprise there."

Keisha had told Gulliver all about the bad side of foster care. There were good sides too. He knew that. Keisha knew that. Only Keisha hadn't gotten much of the good.

Patrick said, "Some kids just can't adjust."

"Or maybe he just missed his dog." Gulliver was curious. "Any leads? Any witnesses?"

"Nope. No one's come forward. No one saw or heard anything. But there aren't always a lot of people down that way."

"You'll keep me posted?"

"Sure. And Dowd," Patrick said, "I know you're a PI. A good one, from what I hear."

"Thanks. But..."

"Stay out of this. This is a police matter. I liked your sister. She was a good cop. But if you get in the middle of this..."

"I understand. I'm on my own. Don't worry. I'm used to that."

Gulliver Dowd had no plans to stay out of it. The people who hired him almost always had money. They could afford to send him out onto the street to look for their missing kids. But who watched out for kids like Ellis Torres? If someone hadn't laid a pipe or a baseball bat across the side of his head, no one would have even noticed him. Not the cops. Not anybody. There were eight million people in New York City. Really, more like ten million. Many of those people were faceless. Nameless. Powerless. No one watched out for them. But not Ellis Torres. Not anymore. He had Gulliver Dowd to stand up for him.

The yellow crime-scene tape was still up. It was blowing in the breeze off the water. The empty ocean container was no more than a hundred yards from where he had met the kid. Valentino Pier was just ahead. But Gulliver wasn't interested in looking at the harbor sights. Not today.

This was the part of the Red Hook that was still rough at the edges. Where the water slapped up against the concrete seawalls. Against old piers. The streets around here were lined with warehouses. Some were full. Some had been empty for years. There were small factory buildings. Tour-bus yards. School-bus yards. Ocean-container storage yards. Some of the streets were still paved with cobbles. Some had old trolley tracks. There was a new pier close by. Some ocean liners docked there. But the docks weren't busy. Not like in the old days.

Ugly pulled on his new leash as they approached the container. His tail wagged like crazy. The dog smelled the kid's scent. As they got close, Gulliver's stomach knotted up again. There was dried blood on the pavement. The spot where they had found the kid. Gulliver took a quick look around. There were some houses mixed in among the warehouses and storage yards. Not many.

He told Ugly to be quiet. Then he did a breathing technique his karate sensei had taught him. It slowed down his breathing. His heart rate. He shut all the noise out of his head. He put himself into a kind of trance. It let him focus. He took a more careful look around. It was as if he was taking photos with his mind.

Ugly wasn't big on trances. He pulled hard at his leash. He barked at Gulliver. He tugged Gulliver in another direction. Down Ferris toward Coffey Street. Past Coffey Street. Past Dikeman to Wolcott Street. He thought the dog must be following the kid's scent. Ugly stopped by a cyclone fence in front of a big beige warehouse. There was a warehouse just like it on the next block. But that one was fixed up like new. Not this one.

Gulliver knew this place. He had seen it on some of his walks. A real-estate firm had had big plans for it. They were going to turn it into condos with harbor views.

They had hired a builder to gut the inside. To redo the outside. But then the real-estate market crashed. The firm ran out of money. The warehouse had sat untouched for the last four years. Some of its concrete skin had peeled away. Some of its steel bones were showing.

Ugly was barking like mad. Jumping up on his hind legs. Spinning around in circles.

"You don't look like a ballet dancer," Gulliver said, "but you sure act like one. All you need is some funny shoes and a tutu."

Dogs are amazing with smells. They can read scents the way people read words. But Gulliver couldn't understand what Ugly was trying to tell him. He bet Ellis Torres would know.

"Come on, Ugly." He tugged on the dog's leash. "Let's take a look around."

They began to walk the four sides of the empty warehouse. Then the skies opened up. Bolts of lightning like neon spider webs flashed across the clouds. Thunder cracked.

Big drops of rain poured down on them.
Gulliver wasn't ready for this. Ugly pulled
on the leash. Gulliver followed. Around
the corner there was a hole in the fence
surrounding the building. On the other
side of the hole was a metal door. The door
was closed. But it wasn't locked. When
he tried the handle, it opened. Not a lot.
Just enough to let a dog and someone
as small as Gulliver inside.

It was dim, but there was just enough
light coming through the windows to see
okay. Gulliver let go of Ugly's leash.

"Go!" he said.

Off went the dog.

The floor was covered in dust. In bits
of chipped concrete. There were old
newspapers lying around. Forgotten tools
here and there. He could see all the way
up to the ceiling high above him. The
builders had taken out all the old floors and
inner walls. They'd taken out the pipes
and wires. Now only metal girders were left.

Gulliver caught up to Ugly. He was in the far corner of the warehouse. This was where Ellis Torres and his dog had lived until yesterday. The kid had made a pretty nice setup for the two of them. There was a mattress. A sheet and a heavy quilt on top. A propane heater. A beat-up Coleman stove. Two LED lanterns. A mirror. A small cooler. A bed for Ugly made out of rags. A case of bottled water. A washbasin made from an old sink. Some dishes and plastic silverware. Towels. A dresser held together with duct tape. Soap. Toothpaste. A toothbrush. Even some books. A ladder leaned against the wall. Gulliver guessed the kid used it for shelving. On the floor around the ladder were some photos. Ellis's mother. *Attractive*. Ellis in a school uniform. That big smile on his face. Ellis holding Ugly as a puppy. The dog wasn't any cuter then. Gulliver was always amazed at how street kids made lives for themselves. Often out of the scraps of other people's lives.

Something about the ladder got Gulliver's attention. But before he could figure out what, his cell phone buzzed in his pocket. It was the vet clinic calling.

"Gulliver Dowd," he answered.

"Hi, Mr. Dowd. This is Mia from Dr. Prentice's office."

He remembered Mia very well. How pretty she was. How she had looked at him. He liked the way she had looked at him. But he had felt a twinge of pain too. He remembered how a girl in college had looked at him and his handsome face with pity. *What a waste*, the girl had said. *What a waste*. That memory haunted him. He hated pity more than anything else, but he's never let it hold him back.

"Please call me Gulliver. What can I do for you, Mia?"

"Dr. Prentice needs to see you. It's about your dog, Ugly."

Instantly he was worried. "Is there something wrong?"

"I'm not sure. The doctor says he needs to see you. Please come into the office, Mr. Dow—Gulliver. As soon as you can."

"Ten minutes okay?"

"That would be great," she said. A smile in her voice. "I'll tell the doctor."

Gulliver grabbed Ugly's leash and said to the dog, "That was a weird call. Maybe the vet's going to tell me you're part alien after all."

CHAPTER FIVE

He wasn't far off. Ugly wasn't from another planet. But something the vet had found on him was from a strange place. A faraway place. Prentice pulled up a two-step ladder for Gulliver to stand on and asked him to look into the microscope.

"It looks like a bug," Gulliver said.

Prentice nodded. "Yes, Mr. Dowd. It's a bug. A very odd insect."

Gulliver was confused. "So what, Doc? The dog must have been covered in all sorts of things. That's why I brought him in here. So you guys could clean him off and fix him up."

"He was in pretty good shape," Prentice said. "Dirty. Smelly. Full of fleas and such. But still in pretty good shape."

"Then what's the problem, Doc?"

"Come with me, Mr. Dowd."

Gulliver followed Prentice into his office. The vet sat down behind his desk. He tapped out something on his computer keyboard.

"Ah. Here we go," he said, turning the screen to face Gulliver. "See that insect there?" He pointed at the picture on the screen.

"That flea? Is that what was on Ugly?"

"Well, no, Mr. Dowd. It isn't a flea at all. It is a flea beetle."

"So it's a flea beetle. What am I not seeing?"

"Flea beetles are common enough, Mr. Dowd...but not in New York."

"What?"

"That's right. We found a few dead flea-beetle larvae on Ugly. I had to call a friend at Cornell to help me identify this insect. Even more strange is that flea beetles are leaf eaters. Odd that I should find them in the fur of a Brooklyn street dog."

"That doesn't make any sense. Like I told Mia, Ugly belongs to a kid named Ellis Torres. I found the dog for him as a favor. I figured I would get the dog fixed up before I gave him back."

"I have to ask. Is there any chance this dog has been to India within the last few weeks?"

Gulliver laughed. "C'mon, Doc. Are you joking? I just told you—"

"I know. But I have to report this to the U.S. Department of Agriculture. It would be a very bad thing if these insects took hold here." The vet cleared his throat. "Is there a chance I could talk to this Ellis Torres boy? I assume he hasn't been to India either."

"My guess is he hasn't even been out of Red Hook. You can ask him yourself. Just not yet."

"What does that mean?"

Gulliver explained about the kid getting whacked in the head. "He's in Brooklyn University Hospital. And last I heard, he was still not awake. You can talk to Detective Patrick at the seventy-sixth precinct if you want more info. But that's all I know."

Dr. Prentice shook his head. "Very odd. Very odd."

"I agree. But right now, I've got bigger things to worry about."

"All right, Mr. Dowd. Thank you for coming back in. I will be in touch if I need to speak to you or see you again."

In the outer office, Mia stopped Gulliver. She was taller than him, though she was no more than five feet herself. She was pretty too, in a way he liked very much. Which was to say she looked nothing like Nina. Nina was dark. Curvy. Husky-voiced. Mia was petite. Blond. Fair-skinned. Her eyes were blue and earnest. When she got on her knees to rub Ugly's belly,

Gulliver saw just how pretty she was. He hadn't been able to get the way she'd looked at him out of his head.

Ugly was even uglier when he was happy. And when Mia scratched his belly, he got very happy. His crooked tongue stuck out. His eyes got bulgier. And his belly sagged to one side. At least God had the same sense of humor with dogs as with humans.

Mia looked at Gulliver and said, "I'm sorry I had to bother you. Dr. Prentice wouldn't stop asking me to call you. He was in a hurry to get you in. To speak with you."

"It's okay. I'm glad I got to see you again...even if you only love me for my ugly dog." He smiled at her in a way he almost never smiled at anyone.

"He's not so bad, really. Besides, it's not Ugly I want to ask to dinner."

"You're asking me to dinner?" Gulliver was shocked.

"I am," she said.

His heart thumped hard in his chest. "Tonight?"

"Tomorrow is better."

His smile got bigger. "Tomorrow then. Should I come get you?"

"I'll come by for you, if that's okay?"

"Fine." He gave her his card. "What time?"

"Seven thirty?"

"See you then," he said.

She brushed the back of her hand against his cheek. "I'm looking forward to it."

Ugly was so happy, he was almost purring like a cat. Gulliver too.

CHAPTER SIX

Gulliver took Ugly to the loft. He had to admit, the dog was good company. But he didn't want his focus divided. He was going back to Ferris Street to ask about the kid. He knew there were things people wouldn't tell the cops. Some people didn't like cops. Or trust them. And some cops could be bullies. No one liked bullies. Gulliver knew that all too well. Until he got out of high school, he'd spent every day of his life being bullied. Cops aside, many folks just didn't think that what other people did was any of their affair.

There was stuff people might tell a private detective that they wouldn't tell the cops. PIs wanted answers, not arrests. And there was something Gulliver could do that the cops couldn't. He could spread cash around. It was amazing how a little money improved people's memories. Sure, people lied for the money. Some people lied no matter what. But there were times when money helped cut through all that. A good PI knew how to sort the lies from the truth. And Gulliver was a really good PI.

Ferris Street was like any other street by the docks. What happened here happened behind warehouse walls. Or factory walls. Or fences with razor wire. You couldn't tell much by looking in from the outside. The only things you could see from the street were trucks or cars passing in and out of driveways. Gulliver decided to start by knocking on the doors of the few apartments and private houses scattered among the businesses.

The first two he tried got him nowhere. Either nobody was home or nobody answered. People didn't like coming to the door for strangers. And Gulliver Dowd was stranger than most. He understood that. There were times he'd seen folks peeking out at him from behind curtains or window shades.

He felt good about the third door. There was a big water bowl on the stoop. Cat and dog food on paper plates on the welcome mat. Whoever lived here had a soft heart for strays. He was willing to bet that Ugly had eaten more than one meal here. An old woman came to the door when he knocked.

"What can I do fer ya, boyo?" she asked in an Irish lilt. She had a mop of white hair. Her skin was wrinkled and spotted with age. But her green eyes sparkled like a child's.

He gave her a business card and introduced himself.

"A real private investigator. Yer jokin'. Yer such a wee slip of man."

Gulliver winked. "Mustn't judge the gift by the wrapping, mother," he said in his best Irish accent.

It was weird how Gulliver's looks helped him do his job. His lack of height. His uneven legs. His too-large head. The things that often made his life a struggle worked for him in his job. His looks threw people off-balance. They didn't know what to make of him. That put him at an advantage. And for some reason, strangers didn't like lying to him.

"Yer right, Mr. Dowd. Forgive my rudeness. I'm Mary Shea."

"Nice to meet you, Mary Shea."

"So, Mr. Dowd. What is it yer thinkin' I can do fer ya?"

He described Ellis Torres.

She smiled with a mouth full of well-worn teeth and said, "The lad who lives across the ways in the warehouse there?"

"That's him. The boy with the ugly dog."

Her face went cold. "Ugly, is it? Now who is it judgin' the gift by the wrappin'?"

Gulliver raised his palms up. "That's what the kid calls the dog. Ugly."

"Well," she said with a wink, "I suppose the wee bugger is a beastly bastard. Sweet pup though. As the day is long. This food here is for him. But he hasn't been by lately."

Gulliver explained what had happened to Ellis. How he was taking care of Ugly. How he wanted to find out why the kid had been attacked.

Mary Shea crossed herself and mouthed a silent prayer. "Will the lad recover?"

"He should. Would you tell me anything you can about the boy? Any detail, no matter how small. When you first noticed him? When you saw him during the day? His routine? Did you ever talk to him? Did you ever see anyone bother him?"

Mary invited Gulliver in for tea. She talked about her time in Red Hook. "'Twas a mighty rough place." About her late husband.

"Bill worked the docks until the day he passed." Her children and grandchildren. "All moved long ago. Just me here with an empty apartment above." Why she hadn't spoken to the cops. "I've no use for them." When she got around to Ellis Torres, her eyes sparkled again.

"I used to see him with his mother in the neighborhood. I knew the devil got hold of her from time to time. When he showed up at the warehouse, I knew the devil had her again. We played a game, the lad and me. I would leave a bag of food by that hole in the fence. Books to read. He would pretend they came from God. There was always food for the dog on me stoop. I kept one eye out for him. No one caused him trouble. He caused none to others."

Gulliver told her Ellis was lucky to have a guardian angel like her. He was a bit disappointed Mary hadn't given him anything to work with. He stood to go.

Thanked her for the tea. Gave her some money. "For the dog and cat food," he said, pressing the cash into her hand.

She blushed a bit and took it.

She called to him as he hobbled away. "Dowd. That's Irish. Isn't it?"

He turned back to her. "It is. I chose it. I don't know what I am, really. I was adopted."

"Yer a good soul, Gulliver Dowd. Bless ya."

He couldn't speak. He took another step.

"Mr. Dowd."

He turned back. "Yes, Mary."

"You did say to tell ya anything at all. No matter how small the detail."

"I did," he said.

"Well, the other night…"

He stepped toward her. "What about the other night?"

"Somethin' woke me from me sleep. After fifty years I'm used to the sounds of the harbor. This was different. First a truck rumbled down the street. Men were shoutin' at one another.

Then there was some god-awful shrieking. 'Twas ungodly, I tell ya. Echoin' down these streets. Scared the bejeezus out of me." She crossed herself again. "Wailin' like a banshee. Do you know of banshees?"

"I've heard of them. I don't know about them."

"They're omens of death."

"Do you remember which direction the truck went? Where the shrieking came from?" he asked.

"Down by the warehouse," she said. "Do ya suppose the banshees have anything to do with what happened to the boy?"

"I don't know, Mary. But I mean to find out."

The first thing he did after leaving Mary's house was head back to the warehouse. He walked around the whole of the building. At least as much as the streets and fence would allow. Gulliver didn't see anything out of the norm. Certainly no banshees. He liked Mary very much. She was a cool old bird. But he didn't know what to make of her shrieking spirits in the night. She was old. And he'd noticed her hearing wasn't so good. Maybe she was dreaming. Maybe she heard some drunken girls laughing. Or a couple having a fight. In the deep of night. Sound bouncing around concrete and brick walls, Mary still groggy with sleep. It was easy to understand how her mind might play tricks on her.

CHAPTER SEVEN

When he got back to the loft, Gulliver was beat. He had spent the rest of the afternoon on Ferris Street. Homes. Warehouses. Whatever. If it had a door, he knocked on it. If it had a bell, he rang it. Mostly everyone was cool. Eager to help. Happy to talk. Too bad they'd had nothing to say. A lot of guys had seen the kid and his dog—no one who saw Ugly could forget him. *Man, that is one funky-looking animal.* But nobody had come up with anything helpful. Not one person could think of a reason anyone would hurt the kid.

Tired as he was, it felt good to have Ugly there to greet him. When he got this thing with the kid cleared up, he would get a dog. Gulliver would go rescue the runtiest runt at the shelter and make a home for it. Since losing his parents and Keisha, he had forgotten simple joys. He'd forgotten what it was like to have someone happy to see him. To have someone at home he wanted to see. Or maybe he hadn't forgotten at all. Maybe it just hurt to remember.

He took Ugly for a walk. Fed him. Then they curled up on the couch. They fell asleep watching TV.

It was close to seven when he opened his eyes. He was still groggy. But he saw that Ugly had moved onto his blanket on the floor. The dog was still asleep. Gulliver made himself a quick sandwich. Washed. Brushed his teeth. Then he headed downstairs. He had done enough walking for the day. He got into his new van and took off.

His old one had been destroyed the year before. It happened while he was looking for Nina's daughter, Anka. Anka's real father had hoped that blowing up the van would scare Gulliver. Slow him down. Maybe even get him off the case. Not likely. Gulliver often said he was built low to the ground, like a hound. Once he got the scent, he didn't let it go. He laughed. He and Ugly had a lot in common. This new van was great. It was customized with all the special controls that let him drive it with ease, and it also had cool tech stuff the old van hadn't.

He wasn't sure where he was going. He just felt a need to go somewhere. Anywhere. Even though he was a small man, he often felt like the world was closing in on him. Like it was weighing him down. Sometimes he just wanted to get in his van and keep going. To run away. Far away. But he could not escape his problems. Not by running anyway. There would be mirrors to remind him wherever he went. And in the mirror Gulliver Dowd saw the truth of who he was. Of what he was. There was no running from the truth.

He got on the Brooklyn-Queens Expressway and headed west, toward the Brooklyn Bridge. Maybe he would take the bridge to Manhattan. Surprise Rabbi. Show up at his apartment with a bottle of red wine. They would sit and talk. Maybe Rabbi would tell him about all the women he was dating. Rabbi was tall. Movie-star handsome. But he could never find the right woman. In a way, he was lonelier than Gulliver.

Gulliver changed his mind when he saw the sign for Atlantic Avenue. He pulled off the expressway. Found a parking spot. Waddled half a block to University Hospital of Brooklyn. Finding Ellis Torres's room number was easy enough. Too easy. That worried him. Someone had tried to kill the kid after all. The cops should have been more careful. Gulliver's heart raced. He was afraid the cops had left the kid unguarded.

He was right to be afraid. When the elevator doors opened, an alarm was sounding. Nurses and doctors were scrambling. Running to a room at the end of the hall. An announcement came over the loudspeaker: "Code Blue. Code Blue." Uh-oh. A patient's heart had stopped. It was all hands on deck to save his or her life. Was it the kid? What had gone wrong? Would he be okay? Then he saw that medical staff were running in the opposite direction of the kid's room. It wasn't Ellis Torres who needed their help. Gulliver let out a sigh. He relaxed.

The relief didn't last long. He looked down the corridor to where the kid's room was. Just as he had feared, there was no cop guarding the room. And with the Code Blue alarm, no one was paying attention to Ellis Torres. Gulliver hurried as best he could. But he kept bumping into people running the other way. He felt like a salmon swimming against the stream.

Now he noticed something else that really scared him. All the other doors along the corridor were at least partially open. Some were wide-open. The only closed door was the one to Ellis Torres's room. Now Gulliver ran. Or what passed for running.

He had overcome many things in his life. But there were things that all the trying in the world couldn't fix. Uneven legs was one of them. What was just a hobble when he walked was much worse when he ran. It was also hard to keep his balance. But he had to. He had to get to the kid's room fast.

He didn't knock. Instead, he shouldered the door paddle. The door flew back. A big man dressed in hospital scrubs was leaning over Ellis Torres. He was holding a pillow over the kid's face.

The big man turned to look at Gulliver. He had pale white skin. His eyes were such a light blue that they almost didn't have any color at all. He sneered at him. Laughed. As if to say, "What is a little bug like you going to do?" And then he turned back to the kid, pressing the pillow down.

Gulliver thought about shooting the man, but knew he couldn't. Hospital rooms had all sorts of pipes and tanks in the walls. He couldn't risk hitting a compressed-gas line or oxygen tank. He couldn't risk the bullet setting off a fire in a place full of flammable chemicals. And the walls were thin. A stray bullet might pass right through and hit someone in the next room.

Instead, he slid his hand under his jacket and felt for the handle of his knife. Pulled it out of its sheath. Laid the blade along his fingers and palm and reared his arm back. Then let the knife fly. The big man screamed in pain. The knife handle was now sticking out of his right shoulder blade. The back of his scrubs turned wet. Red. Soon the back of the shirt was soaked with blood.

The big man let go of the pillow. He tried to reach the knife and pull it out. He couldn't. He turned away from the kid. Turned to Gulliver. He charged. Gulliver stepped to his right and, as the big man got to him, snapped a side kick at the charging man's thigh. But this guy was good. He, too, had martial-arts training. He blocked Gulliver's kick. Grabbed his leg. Shoved him. Gulliver stumbled backward into a wall. He kept his balance, but it was too late. The wounded man had enough time to escape.

Gulliver was torn. Should he chase Ellis's attacker? Should he see if the kid was all right? In the end, it was an easy choice to make. He threw the pillow off the kid's face. The kid was breathing okay. He checked the pulse. That was strong too. He pressed the call button. He pressed it again. He kept pressing it until someone came.

When the nurse finally arrived, Gulliver was dialing 9-1-1.

CHAPTER EIGHT

Detective Patrick looked as unhappy as Gulliver Dowd felt.

"We did have a uniform guarding the room. They found him unconscious in the stairwell."

"What happened to him?" Gulliver asked.

"Doesn't remember. He took a pretty good knock on the head. Got a bad concussion."

"How about the guy who tried to kill the kid? I'd like to get my knife back."

"Very funny, Dowd. We got him on video leaving the hospital through a side entrance," Patrick said. "There was a car waiting for him. It was a stolen car. Found it in Mill Basin. Motor still running. Seat covered in blood."

"Any leads at all?" Gulliver asked.

"The car's being gone over by the Crime Scene Unit. If there's anything to find, they'll find it. We've alerted all hospitals. Walk-in clinics. Doctor's offices. They have to report anything like a knife wound to us. So where did you say you hit him with the knife?"

"In the right shoulder blade. Got him good. Went in pretty deep. I didn't want to risk killing him by hitting him in the left shoulder blade. Too close to the heart."

Patrick stroked his cheek with his right hand. "I wonder what the kid saw that made it worth trying to kill him a second time."

"Sure bet it involves a lot of money," Gulliver offered. "You don't take the kinds of risks this guy took just for the hell of it. He's good for three counts of attempted murder. Two on the kid and one on a cop. That's a lot of years in prison right there."

Patrick said what they were both thinking. "Drugs. It's gotta be drugs."

Gulliver nodded in agreement. He thought of telling Patrick he'd found out where the kid had set up house. About talking to Mary Shea. About talking to all the people along Ferris Street. But he decided against it. Detective Patrick had warned him to stay out of this. Gulliver couldn't risk the cops stopping his investigation. Not yet. Besides, there really wasn't much for him to tell the detective. Only an old lady's story about a loud truck and screaming banshees. He could only imagine what Patrick would say to that.

"What were you doing here in the first place?" the detective asked.

"I was out for a ride. Then when I saw the exit for the hospital...I decided to stop. It wasn't planned."

"Well, good thing for the kid you stopped by or he'd be dead."

"You going to put more men on the door?" Gulliver asked.

"Better than that. We're moving the kid to another hospital."

"Where?"

"Can't tell you."

"Don't be an ass, Patrick. I just saved the kid's life."

"Smithson Rehab Hospital. Small. Private. Twenty-four-hour police presence. But whatever you do, do not share that info with anyone. Got it?"

"Loud and clear," Gulliver said. "Loud and clear."

CHAPTER NINE

He had trouble sleeping that night. At one point he just gave up. He put the leash on Ugly and went for a walk. The days might have been feeling like spring, but the nights still bit hard like winter. The chill of the early morning rattled Gulliver to his bones. And without any fur, even Ugly was shivering a little.

This was Red Hook at its scariest. When no one was on the street. When the buzzing of cars along the expressway was the only sound you heard. That and the beating of your own heart. When random noises shook you. When a helicopter passing overhead sounded like the end of everything. When menace hid behind each shadow.

It was strange how strong the smell of salt was in the air. Then he realized where they were.

Gulliver hadn't planned on walking the dog to Ferris Street. But that's where they found themselves. He stood in the middle of the road. First looking to his left, toward Valentino Pier. Then to his right, toward King Street.

He stared at Mary Shea's house. He stared at the warehouse where the kid had lived. It was easy at this time of night to see how the old woman could have imagined banshees in such a place. Not much scared Gulliver Dowd. He had proved that earlier. He hadn't flinched when he dealt with the guy trying to kill the kid. The big man was a good two feet taller than he was. More than a hundred pounds of muscle heavier. Gulliver hadn't cared.

He didn't believe in evil. People did bad things. Evil acts. Some people seemed to have nothing but hate inside them. But evil as a thing unto itself wasn't real. Yet... as he stood there on the empty street, he was uneasy. Something was going on here that he didn't understand. And Gulliver didn't think it was as simple as drugs.

A car turned onto Ferris Street. At any other time of day, Gulliver would not have even noticed it. But this wasn't any other time. Maybe the driver had taken a wrong turn. It was easy enough to get lost in Red Hook. All it took was one left where you should have made a right. It had happened to him when Keisha first moved to the area. The streets were winding. They sometimes didn't seem to connect.

The car rolled to a stop. Okay, that made sense. The driver was just trying to figure out where he was. Where he had made the wrong turn. Where he should go next.

"Come on, Ugly," he said to the dog. "This guy's lost. Let's help him get out of this maze."

He took a few steps toward the car, then froze. The front license plate was missing. Through the glare of the headlights he looked at the driver. *Uh-oh*. The driver's face was covered by one of those wool caps that pulls down to protect against cold weather. Gulliver calmly turned and walked in the other direction.

Too late. The squeal of spinning tires filled the night. Gulliver looked over his shoulder to see the car bearing down on him and Ugly. He reached down. Scooped up the dog. Made a dive for the doorway of a small factory building. The car hopped up onto the curb behind him. He rolled to his right behind a brick wall that guarded the factory door. There was a bang. The scraping of metal. More squealing of tires.

The car had missed him by less than a yard. He staggered to his feet. Reached under his jacket for his Sig. But he was having trouble seeing. Things were blurry. His eyes stung. The car disappeared around the corner. Gulliver touched his forehead. It was wet with blood. The blood had dripped into his eyes. He'd smacked his head when he dived for cover. He looked down at Ugly. The dog seemed fine. At least one of them was.

CHAPTER TEN

Wasn't it always the way? That's what Gulliver was asking himself as he looked in the mirror. There was a white bandage on his forehead. Under the bandage were ten stitches. He'd only realized how bad the gash was when he got back to the loft and washed off the blood. Then he saw the damage above his left eye.

He'd wound up at Brooklyn University Hospital for the second time in only a few hours. He told the ER doctor he had fallen down. Which was half true. The part he left out was that it was while someone was trying to kill him. And he hadn't called Detective Patrick. This was personal now.

Gulliver had an interesting romance with the truth. Like everyone else, he lied. Only when he had to. Did he stretch the truth? Did he sometimes leave out parts of the truth? Yes. But mostly he tried not to hide from the truth. How could he? And so here he was again. Looking in the mirror. At the bandage over the stitches. Why couldn't the guy have tried to run him over *after* his date with Mia?

"Poor me," he said to himself, half joking. "I haven't had a date since Nina. Now look at me."

He laughed a sad laugh. But he figured he would be okay. He hoped a few scratches and a bandage wouldn't matter to someone like Mia. He would find out soon enough. The bell rang. Ugly ran to the door, his ratty crooked tail wagging like mad. Gulliver's heart was beating just as fast as Ugly's tail was wagging.

He didn't know what to expect. They hadn't really made any plans. He hadn't been sure how to dress. So he went casual. A light gray sweater over jeans and boots. For most of his life, he hadn't cared much about clothes. What did it matter what he wore? Clothes weren't going to make him tall. Muscular. Normal. But once he was a PI, he got with the program. He understood that dressing well was a way to impress clients.

Gulliver pulled back the door. Mia seemed to have read his mind. She, too, wore a gray sweater over jeans and boots. They looked at each other and laughed. Ugly didn't care. The minute he saw Mia he rolled onto his back. The message was clear. "Rub my belly. Rub my belly." Mia understood dog body language. The first thing she did was rub Ugly's belly for a few minutes.

Ten minutes and one glass of red wine later, they were downstairs. They had decided to drive to Arthur Avenue in the Bronx for Italian. The first little crack in the evening happened then. Gulliver turned left, to where his van was parked. Mia turned right, to her car.

"Where are you going?" she asked.

"To my van," he said.

"You drive?"

The surprise in her voice cut like a knife. He reacted without thinking. "Yeah. I tie my own shoes and cut my own meat too."

She walked up to where he was standing. "God, Gulliver, that's not what I meant. I'm sorry."

"No," he said. "I'm sorry. Yes, I drive. Here's my van."

The drive to the Bronx was going smoothly. Gulliver asked Mia about where she was from. "Roseville, Michigan. Outside of Detroit." How big her family was. "There's five of us. Two big brothers and me." What her parents did for a living.

"It's Detroit. Mom works for GM, Dad for Chrysler." Where she went to school. "Eastern Michigan University." How she wound up in Brooklyn. "I took a wrong turn at Indiana. No, really, I moved here with a boyfriend. It didn't last."

Gulliver asked every question except the one he wanted to ask, which was "Why did you want to go out with someone like me?" He was an adult in every way but one. When it came to love, he was still a scared teenage boy. A boy who could never see himself as worthy of love and caring, things he wanted more than anything. Because he'd never liked himself very much, he could not trust that other people did. The only people whose love he had ever trusted were his parents. Keisha. Rabbi. He had trusted Nina once. Never again.

But Gulliver burned to know. Why had someone so pretty asked him out? Why had a woman who could have any man want him? So when they pulled off the Cross Bronx Expressway onto the streets, he asked the question. He asked in a different way. And it came out all wrong.

"Are your parents…normal?"

"What the hell is that supposed to mean?" Mia's voice was angry.

"No, I mean, physically."

"That's supposed to make me feel better?"

"It's just that…" He hesitated.

"It's that what?"

He wanted to say a million things. But he figured anything he said would make it worse. So he said nothing.

Mia didn't have that problem. "Listen, Gulliver, we all have shit in our lives. Your height doesn't make you that special. I've been lonely. All the men that come into the office are either married or gay. You're handsome. You're the most handsome straight single man that's come into the office in weeks. And when I saw you with what is the ugliest dog in the world…I don't know. I just liked you. I can't explain it better than that. My parents aren't little people. I don't take home strays. I asked you to dinner because I like you."

"I…" He didn't know what to say.

At the next red light, Mia got out of the van. She held the door open and turned to Gulliver. "Tonight's just not going to work. I like you. And if you ask me out again, I'll say yes. But you need to do some thinking between now and then."

"Please don't do this. At least let me take you—"

"I'm all grown up, Gulliver. I cut my own meat and tie my own shoes. I'll get home just fine." She slammed the door shut. But it wasn't an angry slam.

He watched her in his sideview mirror as she walked in the other direction. The light turned green. Cars behind the van honked their horns. He had no choice but to drive ahead. He circled the block a few times. Searched the neighborhood. He couldn't find her. He had made a mess of things again. But something Mia had said kept rattling around in his head. *Your height doesn't make you that special.*

CHAPTER ELEVEN

Not only didn't he sleep, he barely shut his eyes. Yes, he was worried about whether Mia had gotten home safely. He had no address for her. No phone number. No way of checking until she was back at work at the clinic. But it was more than that. Her words were still going round and round in his head. Did he think he was special? Was his handsome face the curse he always made it out to be? He had never thought of things quite that way. He couldn't take it anymore. His head hurt from too much thinking.

Reed Farrel Coleman

Fifteen minutes later, he and Ugly were back doing a post-midnight walk on Ferris Street. This time, Gulliver had brought an LED flashlight with him. It was small but powerful. "Kinda like me," he said to Ugly. *Kinda like Mia.* Mia was much on his mind.

Tonight if a car appeared out of nowhere, he was ready to shoot first and ask questions later. But this wasn't to be an aimless walk. He knew where they were going. Straight to the empty warehouse that Ellis Torres and Ugly had once called home.

The warehouse was spooky. The sound his boots made as they scraped along the dirty floor echoed in the emptiness. The flashlight beam cut deep gashes in the darkness. Ugly pulled hard on his leash. This was home. He didn't need a flashlight to find his way. Gulliver did.

The makeshift apartment the kid had set up for himself and his dog looked different under the harsh light of the beam. But really, nothing had changed.

Everything seemed to be as it had been. The mattress. The coolers. The—*Bang!* Gulliver bumped into something. The ladder. There was something about the ladder. What was it? He struggled to remember. He stepped back and shone the flashlight on it and the photos scattered around its base. He'd thought the kid used it for shelving. But there were dusty, kid-sized footprints on the rungs of the ladder. Footprints that went all the way to the top.

Gulliver let go of Ugly's leash. He checked the ladder to make sure it was sturdy against the wall. Then he climbed the rungs. Slowly. One at a time. At the top rung, he could just barely see out the bottom of a big window. The kid, being a little taller, would have been able to see more. Shining his flashlight out the window, Gulliver saw enough. This back wall of the warehouse was no more than thirty feet from the water. And just beyond the concrete seawall was a dock.

"What did you see here, Ellis Torres?" he whispered to himself. "What did you see?"

He climbed down the ladder. He needed to see the area behind the warehouse in daylight. For that, he would need some help. He sent a text message to Ahmed Foster. Ahmed was a night owl, but even owls were asleep by now. Gulliver didn't expect an answer back until later in the morning. He got Ugly and headed back to Visitation Place.

When he got upstairs, his old-fashioned answering machine was blinking red at him. It was Keisha's answering machine. He could never bring himself to toss it. He pressed the Play button.

"Gulliver, hi." It was Mia. "I'm sure you're sleeping. I just wanted to let you know I got home okay hours ago. I didn't want you to worry. I was scared about calling. That's why it took me until now to do it. I thought you might be mad at me. It was wrong of me to do what I did. I was just frustrated at you because I...because...Listen, here's my number." She pronounced each digit slowly and clearly. "Please call me when you get up. I'm an early riser. Anytime after six is fine. Again, I'm sorry."

He replayed the message. He smiled as he listened. He liked hearing her voice. He looked forward to calling her. He was also happy because now he could finally get some sleep. Ugly didn't need to hear Mia's message for that. The little mutt was already snoring.

CHAPTER TWELVE

His phone was vibrating like mad. And the sun was leaking through his windows. He slapped his hand out onto the nightstand. He grabbed the phone and pulled it toward his ear. He thought it must be Ahmed Foster. Maybe Mia. He hoped it was Mia. It was neither.

"Yeah," he slurred sleepily. "What?"

"The kid's awake," said Detective Patrick.

"Huh?"

"The kid, Ellis Torres. He's awake."

"That's great," Gulliver said, sitting up in bed.

"Kinda." Patrick didn't sound excited.

"What's that supposed to mean?"

"He doesn't remember anything about what happened to him. He doesn't remember a lot of the last few days before it happened. He just keeps asking for his dog."

"Head trauma is bad. There's almost always some memory loss," Gulliver said. "At least the kid can talk."

"I know," Detective Patrick agreed. "I was just kinda hoping—"

"—that he would wake up and solve your case for you."

"Yeah, Dowd. Something like that."

"What time is it?"

Patrick was confused. "It's eight o'clock. Why?"

"Shit! I overslept. I've got some calls to make."

"Go ahead and make them. But be here with the dog at ten. Maybe that ugly pup can jar the kid's memory."

Gulliver hung up without a goodbye. He liked Detective Patrick well enough.

He just didn't like being ordered around. Not by cops. Not by anyone. He got out of bed and found the paper he'd written Mia's number on. His phone vibrated again as soon as he began punching in her number. This time it was Ahmed.

"Yo, Dowd, you texted. What's up?"

"I need your help today," said Gulliver.

"What time? Where?"

"My place at two."

"This a paying gig or a favor, little man?

"Paying."

"Then I will see you at two. Do I need to bring along special equipment?" That was Ahmed's way of asking if Gulliver needed him to pack more than his Glock.

"The usual is fine. But you might not want to wear your best clothes. There may be a little fence climbing involved."

"Later."

Finally Gulliver dialed Mia's number, but he got her voicemail. His heart sank. While he was speaking to Detective Patrick and Ahmed, he'd been thinking up some nice things to say to Mia. It didn't seem right to leave them on voicemail. What he had to tell her he wanted to say to her directly. All he said in his message was that he would call her again later. Maybe stop by the vet clinic to chat.

CHAPTER THIRTEEN

Ugly went out of his mind when he came into Ellis Torres's room. He did flips. Ran circles around the kid's bed. Squealed. Barked. Rolled over. Then the little mutt jumped all the way up onto the bed. The kid was just as happy to see Ugly. But Gulliver could tell that Ellis's head still hurt.

Concussions could be really serious stuff. Gulliver knew just how the kid felt. He had had two himself. Bad ones. He never wanted another. The last one had lasted a long time. He'd had a constant headache for weeks. His thinking was confused. His memory was spotty. His vision got blurry. And when he'd moved too quickly, he got sick to his stomach.

It was amazing to watch the two of them together. It was easy to see why people loved dogs. Sometimes it was harder to see why dogs loved people. Not so with Ellis Torres and Ugly. They were a matched pair. The kid started crying as he squeezed the dog in his arms. But things went wrong when he began rocking back and forth with him. Ellis got sick all over the bed and the dog. Not even that bothered Ugly.

Gulliver. Detective Patrick. Detective Rigo. They all stepped out into the hallway while the nurses cleaned up the mess. The reunion between the kid and the dog had made Rigo a little less nasty. He even shook Gulliver's hand hello.

Patrick eyed the bandage on Gulliver's forehead. "What happened to you?"

"Fell down. Smacked my head. Ten stitches."

"Makes you look tough," Rigo said.

Gulliver joked, "I'd have to grow two feet to look tough."

"Not even then." Patrick shook his head. "Not with that face. You've got the face of an angel."

"Well, I'm the right size."

They all laughed at that.

"So does the kid remember anything else?" Gulliver asked.

"It seems like he's remembering something," Patrick said.

"But then he can't seem to say it," Rigo added.

"I've gotten bonked on the head bad," Gulliver told them. "It can really screw you up."

The nurses came out of the room and told the three men they could go back inside. An African-American nurse with rich black skin like Keisha's pointed at them. "Don't you let that boy get all excited again. You understand me? You do and I'll make you clean up next time."

"Yes, ma'am," they said as one, nodding their heads.

They went back into the kid's room. Ellis was sitting up in bed. He was rubbing Ugly's belly.

"Thank you for finding Ugly, mister," he said to Gulliver. "And you got him all cleaned up and everything."

"Got him fixed up too," said Dowd. "He got all kinds of shots and stuff to protect him."

The kid frowned. "But I got no way to pay you for—"

"Don't worry about that, Ellis. I was happy to do it for you. And I kinda like that dog of yours. He's been real good company for me. I don't look so weird when I'm walking next to him."

Ellis laughed. "That's funny, mister."

"Okay, kid, that's great but—" Rigo began.

Patrick cut him off. "Let the kid and Dowd talk."

Gulliver nodded thanks to Detective Patrick. Then he hopped up on the kid's bed. "Listen, Ellis, I know these detectives have already asked you. But can you remember anything about what happened to you?"

Ellis Torres's face turned red, like he was embarrassed. His eyes darted from the detectives to Gulliver and back to the detectives.

"Guys," Gulliver said, turning to the cops, "can you give Ellis and me a few minutes?"

Rigo didn't like it. He opened his mouth to say something. But Patrick shook his head. "Sure, Dowd," Patrick said. "But only a few minutes."

The detectives left the room.

"Okay, Ellis, they're gone. I know you want to tell me something."

"They would laugh at me. I don't like when people laugh at me. You gonna laugh at me?"

Boy, did Gulliver Dowd understand not liking to be laughed at. He raised his right hand. "I promise I won't laugh at you."

"My memory is kinda, like, stupid. The last thing I remembered before waking up here is…" The kid stopped himself. "It's stupid."

"No, Ellis. Please tell me. Look, I found the place in the warehouse where you and Ugly live. I didn't tell the cops. I won't tell them. I saw the pictures. You made a nice place for you guys. I know it's hard for you to trust people. But please try to trust me."

"The last thing I remember was, like, this crazy screaming. But not like a person screaming. It was like nothing I ever heard before. I was, like, sleeping, you know? And it woke me up. At least, that's what I think I remember."

Gulliver Dowd wasn't laughing. All he could think about was Mary Shea's banshees. "Did you climb up the ladder to look out the window? Did you look out the window to see what was screaming?"

Ellis shrugged his shoulders. "Maybe. I'm not sure what happened. But I remember the crazy screaming."

Later, in the corridor, Gulliver told the detectives about the screaming. They didn't seem to think it was important.

"Maybe the kid's making it up," said Rigo.

Patrick wasn't so sure. "Maybe."

Gulliver didn't tell them about Mary Shea. He didn't tell them about the car that had tried to run him down. He didn't tell them a lot of things. Before he told the cops everything, he needed to see what was up with the back of the warehouse.

Ellis Torres was already asleep when Gulliver went to get Ugly.

CHAPTER FOURTEEN

Ahmed Foster had backed his white Cadillac Escalade down the street to keep anyone from seeing what the two of them were up to. And what they were up to was no good. They had already checked the street and nearby buildings for closed-circuit TV cameras. There were none that they could see. Ahmed's SUV was just to block the view of passersby.

Gulliver took the bolt cutters out of the back of the Caddy and handed them to Ahmed. Both he and Ahmed were wearing latex gloves. Strictly speaking, the two of them were committing a crime.

More than one. Breaking and entering. Destruction of private property. Trespassing. The list would probably grow. Ahmed squeezed the handles of the bolt cutter together. *Snap!* The thick U-shaped steel shackle broke cleanly in half. Gulliver twisted the lock. It fell to the ground.

Ahmed swung the gate open. "After you, little man."

Gulliver went through. Ahmed followed. The first thing they noticed when they got to the back of the warehouse was the smell.

"Man, it stinks bad back in here," said Ahmed.

Gulliver agreed. "Terrible. Like a giant box of kitty litter or something."

"Maybe there's a backed-up sewer around here. I mean, this building looks like nobody's done any work on it in years."

Other than the smell, there wasn't much behind the warehouse. There were some old footprints. There were some drag marks. Some ruts left in the ground. But mostly there was just a slab of cracked concrete. Ahmed went over to the dock that was jutting into the harbor. Checked out the moorings a boat might have tied up to.

"These have gotten some use lately," Ahmed said. "See here. There's some slime growin' on top. But look where the ropes tie around. You can see where the ropes cleaned the slime away down to the metal. Other than that, I can't tell you anything."

Gulliver walked the length of the back of the warehouse. There was nothing else to see. He was disappointed. He had hoped there was an answer here. But there was no answer. Only that terrible smell.

"Come on, Ahmed. Let's get out of here."

They closed the gate behind them. Gulliver replaced the lock. He taped the shackle together where the bolt cutters had snapped it. He set the lock in place so the tape hardly showed.

Gulliver handed Ahmed some cash when they got back in the suv.

"Thank you, Ahmed."

"Anytime, little man. You want me to drop you back at your place?"

"No," he said, then gave Ahmed the address for Dr. Prentice's clinic.

Mia's face lit up when Gulliver stepped through the glass door to the waiting room. The room was crowded with pets and their owners. There was a regal Siamese cat in a harness on a woman's lap. The cat kept sneezing.

"Oh, poor poor Julius," the woman said, wiping the cat's nose with a folded tissue.

Julius Sneezer, Gulliver thought. He laughed to himself.

There was a goofy boxer puppy flopping around on the floor. There was a man holding a plastic case with tiny air holes.

Gulliver couldn't tell what was in the case. To his left was a woman full of piercings and tattoos, holding a cage on her lap. In the cage was a large white macaw. The macaw kept crowning the feathers on its head as it looked around the room.

"What's that guy got in his lap?" Gulliver whispered to Mia as he came to the counter.

"An albino python," she whispered back.

"It's like Noah's ark in here today."

"Dr. Prentice is an exotic-animal specialist. We get all kinds of animals in here. Monkeys. Even bats."

"I'm sorry I missed calling you, but—"

"It's okay," she said. "I shouldn't have been so rough on you last night. I hardly know you and I—"

"Forget it. I came here to tell you that what you said was a good thing. I've been thinking a lot about it. Maybe it was me who shouldn't have said what I said. Would you like to try for a do-over?"

Mia smiled. It was a very pretty smile. "Sure. How about tonight?"

"Same time?" he asked.

"Perfect. You know, Gulliver, I felt bad about something else," she said.

"What?"

"I never asked about Ugly's owner. The kid who got attacked. How is he doing?"

It made Gulliver happy that Mia cared. Maybe there was something they could build together. But he fought hard not to hope. The only thing hope ever did to him was hurt him.

"Oh, the kid's doing much better. I saw him today with the detectives handling his case."

"Does he remember anything about what happened?" she asked.

But before Gulliver could answer, Dr. Prentice interrupted.

"Hello, Mr. Dowd."

"Doctor," Gulliver said. He didn't know how much the vet had heard. He didn't want Mia to get in any trouble over his being there for a visit. "I was just telling Mia about the boy whose dog I brought in the other day."

"Yes, I heard. How is he?" the vet asked.

"Much better. His memories are a little confused. But not totally gone." Then Gulliver remembered the insects Prentice had found on Ugly. "What did the Department of Agriculture have to say about those beetles?"

Mia frowned when Gulliver asked that question. Uh-oh, he thought. He better get out of there before Mia *did* get in trouble.

"Oh, those," Dr. Prentice said, clearing his throat. "Nothing back on those yet. Now, if you'll excuse *us*, Mr. Dowd."

It was clear by the way he said *us* that he meant Mia as well. "Sorry, sure." He waved at Mia. "Later."

As Gulliver turned to go, the boxer puppy leapt at the macaw's cage. The bird let out a terrible squawk. It scared the puppy and everyone else in there. The young boxer fell backward, then scrambled to the other end of the waiting room. The puppy was funny, its paws too big for its body. Just a day or two ago, that would have set Gulliver off. He would have gotten weird about how none of his parts quite fit together either. But not today. Not after Mia smiled at him. He took one more look at the boxer and smiled.

CHAPTER FIFTEEN

Gulliver spent the rest of the afternoon working on a different case. In the wake of Keisha's murder, he had set up a tip hotline. He had used some of his savings and some of Keisha's life-insurance money to set up a reward. At first, there were many phone tips. But as the years went on, there were fewer and fewer. Now hardly any came in. A few a year. Mostly from crazies. People who confessed to anything. People who blamed aliens or Elvis's ghost.

For the first few years, Gulliver shared the tips with the police. Then he stopped. Keisha's murder was still officially an open case.

But even a dead cop's case is pushed to the bottom of the pile when the trail is cold. The first detectives on the case were now both retired. Gulliver had hoped the detectives who took over would see something the others hadn't. Fresh eyes can be good. Nothing came of it. It wasn't that the cops didn't care. They did. Everybody cared. There was just nothing new.

Gulliver had to confess that he himself wasn't as tireless in chasing down leads as he had been. At first, there was no lead he wouldn't follow. No lead he wouldn't push the cops to follow. Once he got his PI license, his carry permit, his knife and fighting training, there was no place he wouldn't go to track down a lead or a suspect. It was a good thing his job paid him well. He had spent a lot of time and money traveling all over to talk to people. He had even gone to Alaska to talk to a retired cop who had worked in Keisha's precinct for a few months.

But, like all the other leads, it came to nothing.

That cop had some crazy theory about a secret plan inside the NYPD. A plot to do away with cops who refused to join a secret society. It turned out that the guy had a very bad record. That he was trouble no matter where he went. He had been transferred fifteen times in twenty years. He had been on medical leave many times. And it wasn't hard to figure out why. He was crazy. When Gulliver talked to other cops who had worked with the guy, they all laughed. *Nuts. Paranoid. Schizo. Loony. Bonkers. Cuckoo. Wack-job. Out there*, was how they described him.

In the last year Gulliver had lost heart. And he had been so busy with his own cases. He knew Keisha would be okay with that. She'd always wanted him to shed his bitterness. To make a life for himself the way she had. He'd wondered what Keisha would think of Mia. That's what got him started looking at his old files on Keisha's murder. And then there was Detective Patrick. It was amazing that of all the detectives in the NYPD, it was Patrick who caught the Ellis Torres case. That happens in life sometimes. Things come together by accident.

So when Gulliver got back to the loft, he took out his old Keisha files. He felt many things. His heart sank at the huge size of the pile. It was nearly as tall as he was. And that wasn't even counting the things he had stored on his computer. Thousands of tips. Hundreds of interviews. All of it leading nowhere. Then deep sadness as he recalled identifying Keisha's body. The horror at the sight of what the bullets had done to her. Then happiness as he recalled how much they had loved each other. It was always the two of them against the world. Then swelling pride for what his sister had done with her life.

He began looking through the files. One by one. What he noticed was that then-Patrol Officer Samuel Patrick's name came up a lot. Not in a bad way. Almost every cop in their precinct had said that Sam Patrick and Keisha were friends. That they were close. Even the psycho in Alaska had mentioned that Keisha and Sam were close.

Gulliver hadn't paid any attention to that before. It made sense. In the past, he hadn't been looking for cops Keisha liked. Not her friends. Not the ones she got along with. No. He had been looking for the ones she didn't like. The ones who gave her a hard time about being black. About being a woman. About being too heavy. About being too tough. About not being tough enough. Yes. When this case was done, he would have to sit down with Detective Patrick. If for no other reason than to be reminded of what was so cool about his sister.

Lost in the files, Gulliver let time slip away. He barely had time to shower and dress before Mia arrived. Only she didn't get there. *Tick...tick...tick.* All of his clocks were digital, but he swore he could hear the seconds ticking into long minutes. Again he went through a bunch of feelings. Let-down. Anger. Worry. He began to beat himself up for having hope. It never failed. Why did he let himself hope? It always ended badly. Then, at 8:12, his house phone rang.

It was Mia. But something was wrong. He felt it even before he heard her voice. And when he heard her voice, there was no doubt.

"Gulliver, listen," she whispered. Her voice was tense. She sounded out of breath.

"Mia! What's wrong?" he shouted into the phone.

"What were you and Dr. Prentice talking about before? About the Department of Agriculture?"

"What's that got to do—"

She cut him off. "Please, just answer."

"Remember the other day when you called? When you told me Dr. Prentice needed to see me as soon as I could get there?"

"Sure I do," she said.

"Well, he wanted to talk to me about some dead bugs he found on Ugly. He said they were rare and that they only came from India. He said he would have to report it to the Department of Agriculture."

There was a moment of silence on the other end of the phone. Then, "Something's not right, Gulliver. I do all the paperwork for those kinds of reports and—"

"Maybe he just called them," Gulliver said.

"If he called, I would still have to do a report. He never asked me to do it. And I'm pretty sure he didn't call them."

"Listen to me carefully, Mia. Has anything been going on lately that's weird or different in your office?"

Again there was quiet on the other end of the phone for a moment. "Dr. Prentice has been very tense since his divorce."

"When was that?"

"A few months ago," Mia said. "He lost a lot of money in the divorce. He even told us he might have to close the office down and join someone else's practice."

"But he didn't close the office. Do you know how he's been able to keep it open?" Gulliver asked.

"All I know is that my paycheck doesn't bounce," she said.

"Okay. Anything else weird? I mean in the last few days."

"He has been really jumpy. Very quick to shout. Maybe that's because of the accident."

"Accident!" Gulliver had raised his voice. "What accident?"

"The other night, Dr. Prentice screwed up his car. He said he was swerving to miss a dog. He hopped up onto the sidewalk and scraped the entire side of his car. It's in the shop."

"But what's wrong with you? Why aren't you here? Why do you sound—"

"After I heard what you and Dr. Prentice were talking about, I knew something was wrong. I decided to come back to the office and look around. I have keys. I knew if I told you what I was doing, you would have told me not to."

"You're damn right. Get out of—"

"I found something," she said. She was breathless again.

"What is it?"

"Cash. An entire file drawer full of bundles of—"

Mia stopped talking, but she didn't hang up. Gulliver heard a file drawer slamming shut. Heard footsteps on a tile floor. Then, "Mia, what are you doing here after hours?" It was Dr. Prentice, and he didn't sound happy.

"I had a date tonight."

"Yes, I heard you and Mr. Dowd talking." Gulliver could hear them. The sound was muted. Maybe Mia had dropped the phone into her bag. Maybe she was holding the phone behind her. "But that doesn't answer my question, Mia. What are you doing here?"

"I was having second thoughts," she said. "I decided I didn't want to go out with him. But I left his card here. I wanted to call to tell him. I'm not the kind of person to just not show up."

Smart girl. She was telling her boss a lie he would believe. After all, who would want to date a little freak?

It didn't work. Prentice's voice got angry. "Did you leave his card in my file cabinet?"

"I don't know—"

"Don't lie to me," he yelled.

"I'm not—"

Then Gulliver heard the sharp sound of a slap.

Mia was crying. "Please don't. Please do—"

That was it. That was the last thing he heard Mia say.

CHAPTER SIXTEEN

Gulliver left his house phone off the hook. He knew that as long as Prentice didn't find Mia's phone, there was a chance to save her. Once he was in his van, it took him less than three minutes to get to the vet clinic. Too late. They were gone. Gulliver knew what his next move was. He would call Detective Patrick. Patrick could use Mia's phone to track her. But just as he was about to use the van's cell-phone hookup, he got an incoming call. It was from Mia's phone.

"Dowd. I think you know who this is." Dr. Prentice's voice echoed in the van.

"Yeah. I know."

"Okay then. I think you know I have something you want."

"Don't hurt her. You hurt her and I'll—"

"You're in no position to threaten me, Dowd. Just do as I say and maybe we will all come out of this in good shape. Maybe."

That was a lie and Gulliver knew it. But he didn't have much choice other than to play along. To stall for time. One way to do that was to be silent. So he sat there, waiting for Prentice to get antsy. As he waited, he quietly flipped up the lid of the van's console. He reached in and got out one of the spare cell phones he kept on hand. There were times he gave phones to informants. Or to runaway kids to call their parents. He had never thought he would need one for something like this.

Prentice got tired of the silence. "Dowd! What are you up to?"

"Nothing. Waiting for you say something." Gulliver spoke as he texted. He sent the text. And said a silent prayer that the person he'd sent it to was there to receive it.

"You're being watched. So don't do anything stupid."

Gulliver didn't know whether Prentice was telling the truth. It didn't matter. The van's windows were tinted darker than was legal. When you're a PI, you have to be able to watch people without being seen. The windows on his van let Gulliver see out. Seeing in was not so easy.

"I'm short. Not stupid."

"Mia will stay alive as long as that stays true. Keep the phone line open, and I'll give you directions," Prentice said.

"Put her on the phone. I want to know she's alive."

"Don't give me orders, Dowd. She's alive." As if on cue, Mia moaned. "You're going to have to take my word for it," Prentice said.

"Where are we going?" Gulliver asked.

"I'm not stupid either, Dowd. The directions will be step by step. You'll know where you are going when you get there. Get on the Gowanus Expressway and head to the Belt Parkway East. Remember. You break this phone connection, and Mia is dead."

"I got it."

As Gulliver drove he looked out to his right. He saw a container ship passing under the Verrazano Bridge. As he continued east, he saw a line of ships waiting to enter New York Harbor. Something clicked for him, seeing those ships. All at once things began to come together. To make sense.

He thought about Mary Shea's shrieking banshees. He thought about Ellis Torres saying that screaming had woken him from sleep. In his head he heard the macaw squawking. He recalled how the area at the back of the warehouse smelled like giant kitty litter. How Ahmed had said that the dock behind the warehouse had been used.

"The cops think this is about smuggling drugs," Gulliver said to Dr. Prentice. "But it isn't about drugs at all. It's about exotic animals."

There was silence from Prentice. Then, "I don't know what you're talking about. Just shut up and keep driving. Get off at the Flatbush Avenue exit that leads into Brooklyn, not to Rockaway."

Gulliver had no intention of shutting up. "Mia told me you're an expert on exotic animals. It all makes sense now. I spoke to a witness who said she heard a truck rumble down Ferris Street. She also said she heard shrieking late at night. Like banshees, she said. I dismissed her too quickly. But when Ellis Torres told me the same thing…"

"Shut up, Dowd. You're coming to the exit."

Gulliver got off the exit. "Sure, it was animals. That's why you hurt the kid. You thought the warehouse was empty. He saw you off-loading on the dock. If he had just stayed in the warehouse, he would have been okay. But he went outside to get a better look. You guys spotted him. He took off and you caught up to him by Valentino Pier. That's when you cracked him across the head."

"Shut up," Prentice shouted. "Just shut up! Turn right onto Avenue U."

"How did you get the animals onto—"

Gulliver heard another sharp smack. Mia moaned.

Prentice screamed into the phone, "Not another word, Dowd. Open up your mouth again and I'll kill her."

Gulliver Dowd didn't have to be told twice.

121

CHAPTER SEVENTEEN

F ive minutes later Gulliver was driving
through the gates of the Kings County
Yacht Club. The club was in the Mill Basin
section of Brooklyn. Mill Basin, where the
cops had found the car the big man used
to escape. It was a well-to-do area that
had access to Jamaica Bay and the Atlantic
Ocean. In another month the club would
be busy. People would be getting their
boats ready for warm weather. But now
the club was deserted. Only two other cars
were in the parking lot.

Prentice told Gulliver to park his van.
To get out and walk to dock number 112.

Gulliver did as he was told. He didn't like walking into a spot like this. A strange place. In the dark. He was dealing with a man who had a lot to lose. Gulliver didn't know if Prentice was armed. And Prentice had Mia.

Gulliver didn't know much about boats. He didn't have to. But it was clear that the boat at dock 112 cost a lot of money. It was at least forty feet long. The name painted on her was *El Condor*. It figured. He could hear the low purr of the boat's motor.

Gulliver's stomach knotted up as he got closer to *El Condor*. It wasn't Dr. Prentice waiting for him on the deck. It wasn't Mia. It was the big man. The one with the light blue eyes. The one who had tried to smother Ellis Torres. And the look on the big man's face wasn't friendly. Why would it be? Gulliver had thrown a knife deep into the man's back. And there was something else. The big man was holding a MP5 machine pistol.

Gulliver stopped in his tracks. He was at the end of the dock. Thirty feet behind the aft end of the boat. He took a few steps back. This put a smaller boat and a tall post between himself and the big man.

"Why do you stop?" The big man had a German accent. "You will come here."

"I will not come anywhere," Gulliver shouted back. "I want to see Mia and Prentice on the deck."

"Little insect. You do not give orders."

Gulliver now wished he had thrown the knife through the big man's left shoulder. Right into his heart. If he had one. Gulliver doubted Prentice would have been so bold if this big guy were dead. He thought about taking a shot at the man. He decided against it. Both the MP5 and his Sig were 9mms. The problem was that the MP5 could shoot hundreds of rounds a minute. As good as the Sig was, it could not compete with that.

"How's your shoulder feeling, Franz?" Gulliver called to him.

"I am not Franz, insect. I should have made you dead in the room of the hospital for what you did."

"And I should have thrown the knife through your neck. So we're even, Franz."

"I am not Franz! I am Hugo!" the German was shouting when Prentice came on deck.

"Hugo. Idiot! What are you screaming about?" Prentice was seething.

"Let me kill this insect now," Hugo said to Prentice. "Better to kill him now."

Prentice whispered something in Hugo's ear. Not good, Gulliver thought. Not good. He didn't wait for Hugo to start shooting. He reached for his Sig. Hit the ground. And not a second too soon. There was a stream of fire spitting from the barrel of the MP5. Wood splintered above Gulliver's head. Bullets shattered the fiberglass hull of the boat he had taken cover behind.

Gulliver moved to his right. Lined up a shot. Squeezed the trigger. The shot missed. But it was close enough to the big man's head to make him take notice. Hugo and Prentice got down and flattened themselves to the deck of *El Condor*. Prentice crawled away and disappeared below deck. Gulliver looked around for his help to arrive. But he saw no one. Heard nothing.

"Time to make you dead, insect," Hugo shouted as he got to his feet. He put a new clip in the MP5. He hopped down from the boat and onto the dock. He walked toward Dowd. As he did, he aimed short bursts of fire at Gulliver. More wood splinters. More fiberglass shards.

Being stuck flat on the ground wasn't such a great place for Gulliver to be now. He shot back a few rounds at a time. Not so much to try and hit the big man but to buy himself some time. To give himself a chance to get up. To retreat. It was no good. There was really no place for Gulliver to hide. And his running was woeful. The big man was closing in. Gulliver wheeled around to squeeze off his last few bullets. But when he spun, Hugo's gun had already gone silent.

The big man was on the ground. He was twitching. Grunting. Flailing his arms and legs. He had been Tasered. Gulliver breathed a sigh of relief. His help had arrived at last. A figure dressed in matte black clothing stepped out of the shadows. Ahmed Foster.

Ahmed bent over the big man. Gulliver couldn't see what Ahmed was doing. But when Ahmed stood up, Hugo was no longer twitching. He was no longer doing much of anything.

"Is he dead?" Gulliver asked.

Ahmed shook his head no and whispered, "Let's just say he's asleep and he's gonna be that way for a while."

"Remind me to thank the navy for your SEAL training."

"Where's the girl at?"

Gulliver pointed at *El Condor*. "My guess is she's below decks."

Ahmed picked up Hugo's MP5. Ejected the old clip. Put in a fresh one. He handed it to Gulliver. "You know how to use this?"

"I'll figure it out."

"Get the other guy up on deck. Whatever you got to do. Just get him on deck," Ahmed said. Then he slipped back into the shadows. A few seconds later, Gulliver heard a quiet splash in the water.

He walked back to *El Condor*. "Prentice! Get out here," he yelled. "Hugo's not in any shape to help you. Get out here. We need to talk. All I want is Mia. Give Mia to me and you can get gone."

He felt panic rising in him when there was no answer. In spite of the chill, sweat was soaking through his shirt. The only sound was the slapping of water against the dock. The purr of *El Condor*'s engines. Then there were footsteps. Two sets of them.

Prentice and Mia were on deck. Mia's face was swollen. One of her eyes was bruised. Her lip was cut and bleeding. Her hands were tied together with tape. She was shaking. She was scared. She had reason to be. Prentice held a shotgun under her chin. He looked scared too. His eyes were wide. He was breathing fast.

"Where's Hugo?" Prentice asked.

"He's dead," Gulliver lied. "You're alone now, Doc."

"I have her." The vet tilted his head at Mia.

"Give her to me. Take your boat and go."

"Drop the gun, Dowd. Drop it."

"No, Doc, I don't think I will."

Prentice shoved the shotgun hard into Mia's neck. She almost fell over. "I'll kill her."

"And then I'll kill you," Gulliver said. "And I'll do it very slowly. You dug my knife out of Hugo's back. I threw that one. With one in my hand...I am very good with a knife, Doc."

"You little bastard," Prentice shouted. "You screwed this all up. You and that stupid kid."

"Let's forget all that. Let's deal with what we've got to deal with now. I'm giving you an out. Just push Mia onto the dock. Then get out of here. It's the best deal you're gonna get. At least you get to live. Who knows, maybe you'll get away. You've got plenty of cash."

Gulliver had painted Prentice into a corner. And Prentice's fear was turning into panic. The vet was finding out that real life wasn't like TV.

"Put your gun down, Dowd. I'm going to kill her! I am!" He used his free hand to shove Mia onto her knees.

Prentice was about to find out that that was a very big mistake. At that second Ahmed thumped the hull of *El Condor*. The vet swung his shotgun around. Already on her knees, Mia leaned forward. She crashed to the dock shoulder first. Before Prentice could swing the shotgun back around, Gulliver pulled the MP5's trigger. Prentice's knees shattered. He screamed in pain. The shotgun fell out of his hands and into the water. He crumpled to the boat deck. Then headfirst, with a thud, onto the dock.

By the time Ahmed lifted himself out of the water, Gulliver had cut the tape from Mia's wrists. He was cradling her in his arms. Short as they were, Gulliver's arms felt like the safest arms in the world to Mia.

"She all right?" Ahmed asked.

"I'm fine," Mia said. "Thanks to you two."

"I'm going to call nine-one-one," Ahmed told Dowd, and he headed to the parking lot.

"We do have some strange dates," Mia said.

"Maybe someday we'll even get to eat dinner," Gulliver said.

They laughed. And they held each other until the police came.

CHAPTER EIGHTEEN

Two weeks later, Detective Sam Patrick and Gulliver Dowd were at an outdoor café in Red Hook. Ugly slept by Dowd's feet. It was warm. The sun strong. The skies clear, as they were the day Ellis Torres had run into Gulliver on Valentino Pier. But almost everything else had changed. Mia's bruises had faded. She had a new job. Gulliver and Mia had eaten dinner together every evening since that night at the yacht club.

"The kid gets out of the hospital today," Patrick said. "He's got to go into foster care until his mom gets out. I hope he doesn't run again."

Gulliver shielded his eyes from the sun. "He won't. We talked about it. Last time, he ran because of the dog. I'm taking care of Ugly until he and his mom can get back to being a family. You know that old lady I told you about. She's got an empty apartment they can live in. There'll be someone around to keep an eye on the mom and the kid."

"Your pal Dr. Prentice won't be getting out of the hospital anytime soon. You shot up his knees pretty bad."

"I'll send him a get-well card," Gulliver joked. "Is he still not talking?"

"No. That's why I asked to meet you here. I wanted to tell you. His lawyer cut a deal with the Brooklyn DA and the Feds. He confessed to it all. You were right, Dowd. He and Hugo were smuggling rare animals into the States. Some were for private zoos. Some were for rich-men hunting clubs. How sick is that?"

"It must have paid well."

"Millions," said the detective. "They would take the boat out to meet cargo ships waiting to come into the harbor. Then they would off-load the animals from Prentice's boat in Red Hook behind the warehouse. From there they would take them to his office. He would check them out. Give them whatever shots they needed. Then they would be trucked to the zoo or the club."

"What went wrong?" Gulliver asked.

"The animals were all supposed to be knocked out with drugs."

"But the night the kid woke up the animals woke up too."

"Right," Patrick said. "The drugs wore off too fast. And it was a shipment of monkeys. I guess the monkeys were pretty pissed off after a long ocean voyage.

They musta been screaming their heads off. What I don't figure is why Prentice fed you that story about the Indian beetles."

Gulliver laughed. "He wanted to know if the kid would live. Also if you and Rigo were making progress on the case. I was Prentice's only source. He had to get me into his office somehow."

"It was still dumb, because it got you curious."

"It's my height. People underestimate me all the time. Because I'm little, they think I'm stupid. Or deaf. Or weak."

"You're none of those, Dowd. But you should have kept me in the loop."

"Sorry about that. I'm stubborn that way. I've gotten too used to doing stuff my way."

"Forget it." Detective Patrick's cell rang. "I've got to take this," he said. "Hang around. It will only take a minute."

"Nah," said Gulliver. "It's a beautiful day. I'm going to take a walk over to Valentino Pier."

With that he stood up. Tugged on Ugly's leash. And the two of them were gone.

ACKNOWLEDGMENTS

Thanks to Bob Tyrrell, David Hale Smith, and Sara J. Henry. Special thanks to Rosanne, Kaitlin, and Dylan. Without them none of this would be worth it.

Called a "hard-boiled poet" by NPR's Maureen Corrigan and "the noir poet laureate" in the *Huffington Post*, **REED FARREL COLEMAN** has published seventeen novels. He is a three-time recipient of the Shamus Award for Best PI Novel of the Year and is a two-time Edgar Award nominee. He is an adjunct instructor of English at Hofstra University and lives with his family on Long Island. For more information, visit www.reedcoleman.com.